Solomon's

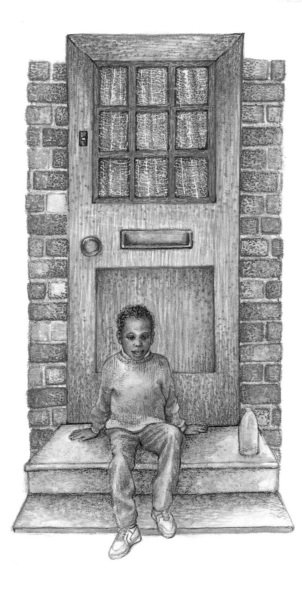

To Martin Cowell and Vicki
HC
To Margaret Andrews
SP

Solomon's Secret

Saviour Pirotta & Helen Cooper

METHUEN CHILDREN'S BOOKS · LONDON

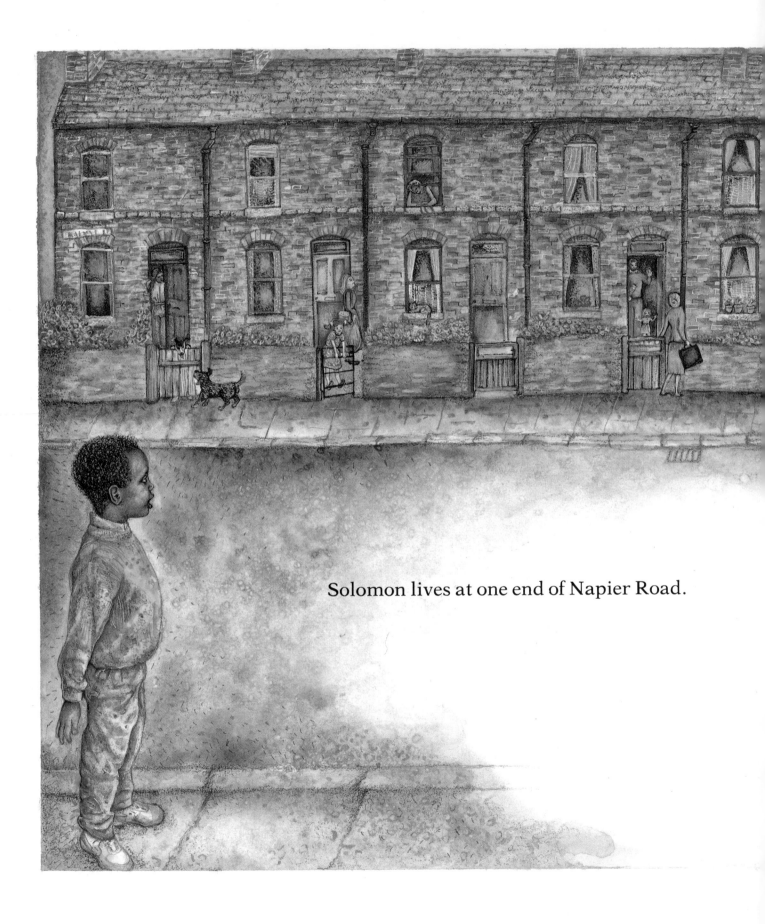

Solomon lives at one end of Napier Road.

Mr and Mrs Zee live at the other end.
The Zees like to keep to themselves. Mrs Zee only
comes out of the house once a week to water
the rhubarb. Mr Zee just sits indoors and plays
his harmonica.

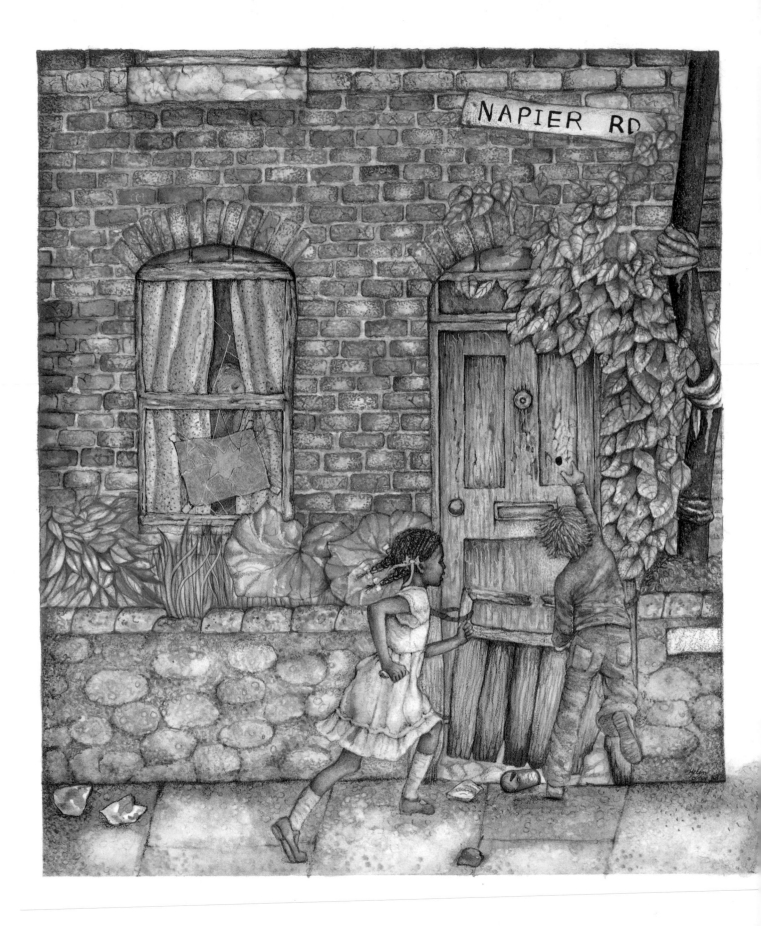

Sometimes Solomon's friends throw stones at the Zees' front door.
'Mrs Zee is a vampire,' Lorna calls, 'That's why she never goes shopping.'
'And Mr Zee is a werewolf,' echoes Stan, 'He only comes out in the dark.'

But Solomon never takes part in these games.
For Solomon and the Zees share a wonderful secret . . .

It all started last summer.
Dad and Solomon had just baked some lovely
apple tarts with cream.
'Why don't we give some to the Zees?' Dad said,
'I'm sure they'd like them.
You can take them round, Solomon.'

Dad put some tarts on a plate and
covered them with a napkin.
Solomon did not want to go,
but Dad insisted.

Ding dong. Mrs Zee answered the door.
'Ooh, Solomon,' she said, 'Come in.'

Mrs Zee introduced Solomon to Mr Zee. 'Delighted to meet you,' said Mr Zee. 'Won't you stay for tea?'

Mrs Zee laid out the table. 'What could we have with the apple tarts?' she wondered.

'Pumpkin pie would do nicely,' said Mr Zee. 'With a pot of China tea and some Indian jalebis for afters. Come on Solomon. We must fetch them before the kettle boils.'

Mr Zee led Solomon through a creaky door
into the garden.
Solomon had never seen such tall rhubarb stalks before.
'What are we looking for?' he asked.
'A trail of pawprints,' said Mr Zee. 'Not dog's pawprints,
of course. Those will only take us round and round the garden.
What we need is something that will take us further –
something like a trail of Panda pawprints.'

Solomon found a panda pawprint beneath the branches
of a willow tree.
'The trail starts here,' said Mr Zee. 'We'd better hurry.
We mustn't keep Lin Ho waiting.'

Solomon trotted after Mr Zee.
The panda trail stretched all the way through the rhubarb
stalks, past a huge mountain, and over a bridge covered
in willows.

At the other end of it there was a small village with
children playing on the streets.

'Welcome to China,' said Lin Ho. 'Here is your tea.'
'Thank you,' said Mr Zee. He paid Lin Ho and led Solomon
back along the trail to the rhubarb garden.

'Now we need a trail of Tiger pawprints,' he said.
Solomon saw a strange mark in the mud between the
duck pond and the holly bush.
'Could this be it?' he asked Mr Zee.
Mr Zee nodded.

The tiger trail took them across a deep valley, past
a large palace with ivory towers and . . .

. . . down a narrow street with delicious smells wafting out of the windows. 'Tiger trails,' said Mr Zee, 'always lead you to . . .

. . . the best sweetshops in the world.'

'Welcome to India,' said Mrs Rai. 'What will it be
today? Some fresh jalebis?'
'Oooh,' said Solomon. 'They smell delicious. Thank you.
Mrs Rai.'
'That will be ten rupees, please.'

Mr Zee counted out ten rupees and thanked Mrs Rai.
He let Solomon carry the hot jalebis back to the garden.

Soon the two of them were looking for
the tracks of a Roadrunner.
'Here they are,' cried Solomon.

The roadrunner trail took them past some
tall cactus and straight to . . .

. . . a little cake shop in the middle of a desert.
'Best pumpkin pie in the United States for the
gentleman,' said Mr Ronald Best.
'Thank you,' said Mr Zee.

He and Solomon hurried back to the rhubarb garden.

'You're just in time for a nice cup of tea,'
said Mrs Zee. 'Are you hungry?'
'I'm starving,' said Solomon.
Mr Zee helped Solomon lay the pumpkin pies
and the jalebis on the table.

Mrs Zee warmed the teapot and gave everyone
a lovely napkin with patterns round the border.
Mr Zee cut everyone a slice of pumpkin pie.
'You can come again next Saturday,' said Mrs Zee to
Solomon as he tucked into the food. 'But keep this a
secret between us.'
Mr Zee poured Solomon some tea.

'We might find a Green Mamba trail
next time,' he said. 'Who knows where
that might lead?'

First published in Great Britain in 1989
by Methuen Children's Books,
Michelin House, 81 Fulham Road,
London SW3 6RB
Text copyright © 1989 by Saviour Pirotta
Illustrations copyright © 1989 by Helen Coope

Printed in Belgium
by Proost

ISBN 0 416 11262 5